To Kimberly,
In case you aren't already tired of reading my stuff. At least you don't have to grade this one!

happy holidays!

Copyright © 2017 June Rossaert
All rights reserved.

The Unexpected And Highly Misguided Theory of Everything

By June Rossaert
Illustrated by Ioannis Lazaras

For Samuel & Satteva
I love you.

(Don't make this into a thing, I'm a writer, I have to pretend to care about something. Just- Just go with it okay?)

PREFACE: WHY AUGUSTO GIOVANNI D'ELEA MISSED SCHOOL

Fifteen years ago, in the small town of Coanesbury, Ontario, in classroom 33B on the second and highest floor of Zeno Achilles Elementary School situated on the 55th of Maine Street, a young boy raised his hand. His name was Augusto Giovanni d'Elea, but he did not know how pretentious that made him sound. Augusto was twelve years old, had hawkish piercing blue eyes, an outrageous love of bright colours and something of a quality about him that invariably caught (and retained) the attention of those around him. He held, without meaning to, the very vibration of the air around him. One might thus realistically stipulate that he had built himself somewhat of an accidental halo.

Unfortunately for the state of the Universe, Augusto d'Elea was a moron.

Of course, Augusto's teacher, miss McGregor, responded to the interjection immediately, ignoring, in doing so, another child who had stayed quiet despite their inner frustrations. No one had noticed that this girl had been begging for attention for the better part of half an hour: she was not the main character of a third-rate, wildly terrible and enthusiastically uninteresting science fiction novella. Augusto d'Elea, clearing his throat and standing up as the room fell into a deafening silence, said this:

"Miss, I have a moon question." The astronomy section of their science class had concluded over a month ago and yet, the teacher did not immediately stop him for this distraction. Not that the question would have been pertinent even if they had still been in that quarter. This was Augusto, his mind worked in mysterious ways. "So- to walk to end of the room, stay with me it relates to the moon, just wait, so yes, to walk to the end of the room, you always need to walk to halfway through the class first right? And then you have to walk halfway through the other half, and halfway through half of the half, and then halfway through that- forever. So that doesn't make sense because it's always infinity half and you can't walk infinity far… except you can because you could so walk all the way across the class! So you're just walking infinity steps all the time! So it should be just as easy to walk to the moon, right? Since everything's always just half of half of half of everything forever, right?"

Miss McGregor stared at him blankly, wondering how it was that she continuously listened to a boy who was consistently and incredulously incoherent. The rest of the class had a similar reaction.

"Don't be silly Augusto, you can't walk to the moon: There's no bridge."

The rest of the class went over without a hitch, and Augusto remained as confused as he'd always been. Nothing made any sense, but he supposed that was the way things were.

However, that very afternoon, while walking home from school, Augusto tripped. And in that instant, the Universe made up for all of its endless and tiresome nothings with a great big something. Amidst a shake a sigh, the Universe pulled a spontaneous wormhole under the child's wandering feet. And in the most infuriatingly and inexcusably brilliant of coincidences, the child fell directly on an incredibly small, blueish moon situated 2.5 million light years away from earth.

This moon orbited a strange, indigo-red planet whose atmosphere was coincidentally very similar to that of earth, mostly because the author was too lazy to think up a more interesting contraption to excuse Augusto's survival. The child was soon found by the inhabitants of the moon, and rapidly sent to the moon's single orphanage. It was then due to his incredible talent of appeal, which graciously seemed to extend to most aliens, that he was promptly adopted by a loving family of Gorgonite immigrants who lived on-planet.

And thus, finally, Augusto Giovanni d'Elea became the first human to ever set foot on planet Number Five.

INTERLUDE IN E MINOR

When the forgotten rise,
they turn their skin off.
The spinal breath of the cursed,
brews luck from the broken pot.
And in a cruel joke of the absurd,

[we walk the moon]

So fuck your bridges.

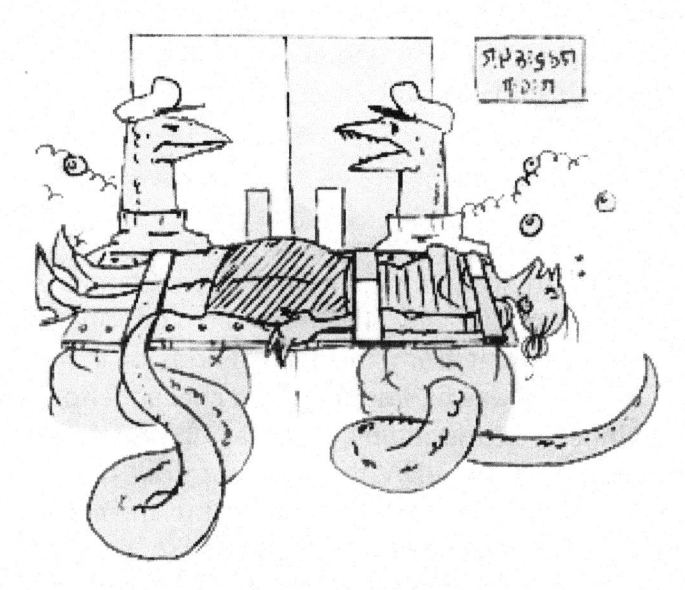

ON LIZARDS AND SONAR DEFICIENCIES

When Gemma Noelle Gott woke up, she could only presume that she was in the middle of an involuntary acid trip and that it was going very, very wrong. Her small feet were strung up in a banana-yellow tree whose pear-shaped, multicoloured fruits shined in a way that much resembled polished metal, and there appeared to be an entire forest of them. The ground was purple and vaguely mobile as well as strangely translucent, forming a gelatinous texture which did little to reassure the woman.

The sky was orange and blue, melting together as one under the light of its three suns. A single moon ran across most of the skyline, seeming almost close enough to touch, a family of odd creatures looked up at Gemma from the ground near the edge of the forest. They appeared somewhat concerned and entirely terrifying, their bodies covered in orange fur. The family looked somewhat giraffe-like, and most traumatically, had five small hooves at the end of each leg.

Gemma was an elementary school teacher and, as far as she could remember, she had been on her way to work a few seconds earlier. She hence found this entire situation quite difficult to process. Somewhere in the back of her deeply shell-shocked mind, she decided that the best way to handle the situation was to scream as loud as she could and pass out.

So she did.

———

Stonesburg's Youth Academy in Ontario, where Gemma worked, had a stellar reputation. One which Gemma had a difficulty living up to. As a recent immigrant from the far confines of a small town in northern Texas, she was finding it quite a challenge to adapt to the large Canadian metropolitan, especially where her teaching credentials were concerned. At thirty-six years old, Gemma had a fair bit of experience teaching the third grade, but the material she had to cover to satisfy this new administration was somewhat beyond her level of expertise. These were children of the Ontario elite. Children whose parents seemingly expected their kids to understand the basics of nuclear physics by the time they entered kindergarten.

Gemma Noelle Gott had never known anything about nuclear physics.

The young woman had been becoming increasingly demoralised by the steadily intensifying parent-teacher interviews. The parents, who had been hesitant at first, gradually came to resemble an angry mob, as led by Helen Thatcher, president of the Parent Teacher Association, and presumably part-Gremlin. The woman had what appeared to be a personal vendetta against Gemma, who had over time become painfully aware that her master's degree in education was a dramatic underachievement for Mrs. Thatcher and the other parents.

For the past five years of her life, then, Gemma had grown more and more certain of her own incompetence, which had, in turn, sapped her enthusiasm. While consistent snobbery of her student's guardians had at first strengthened her resolve to prove them wrong, the resulting disrespect of the children had made that task entirely impossible. Having lost all form of authority with the students, they avoided listening to her, and hence did poorly in standardised tests.

Truthfully, she had been on the verge of a burnout for so long that somewhere, deep in her subconscious mind, she wondered if this new situation, her awakening on the planet she would soon learn to call Number Five, could possibly be a complete psychotic breakdown on her part. Her delusion, surely, was her body's way of easing her out of her own personal hell. She believed herself quite creative, then, in coming up with the sheer strange beauty of the artistic landscape surrounding her now-unconscious body.

It did not occur to her that such an absurd turn of events could possibly be real.

———

When Gemma Noelle Gott woke up again, two giant lizards with neon pink uniforms were carrying her on a specifically designed harness which strapped her sideways across both of their backs. They were making their four-legged way towards a skyscraper made of glass adorned with a bright red sign in a language Gemma could not understand. This time, she attempted nothing, convinced as she was that the delusion would fade and bury itself on its own. Thus, she tried her best to stay calm, counting backwards in her mind to keep herself from feeling too powerlessly insane. Ten, nine, she still needed to get to school, eight, seven, she had a load of laundry to do, six, five, she needed to eat lunch, four, three, had she brushed her hair? Two, one, she needed to deconstruct the situation, ten, nine, feel the cool, wet, Ontario air, eight, four, three, six, she needed-

Stop.

The carrying lizards had stopped moving in a single, short, jolting motion. The creatures, who, unbeknownst to Gemma were Reptilian policemen, -policereptiles if you will - stopped before the tall glass doors of the tall glass building. They spoke to each other in an aggressive and somewhat terrifying hissing language which troubled the redheaded woman. The one which held her upper body, Gh'reywinthx Ghhrths, was pondering the morality of their actions, while Mnth'rosfinn Ghhrths, his husband and the one supporting her legs, argued for legality:

"If we take the alien to the national guard, they'll either send it back to its home planet or exterminate it. Mnnth'rosfinn, you know plenty well how difficult circumstances have to be on one's home planet in order for someone to attempt crossing through the galactic border wall!" hissed Gh'reywinthx, unaware of how clumsy his exposition delivery was.

"It's not our job to decide what happens to it, Gh'reywinthx, it's an illegal alien! And for all we know, it's not even an intelligent creature, it could be a space-wanderer who made it out here accidentally which really should be ejected from the ecosystem. It certainly doesn't seem very acclimated to our atmosphere." Argued Mnth'rosfinn, adding to the expositional discussion and pointing with his tail to the sunburns which were growing like spots on Gemma's sensitive Irish skin. He was right, too, the radiation of three suns was a bit much for the freckled woman.

"We could take it to the Refuge? At least they won't exterminate it, and they might help it become a legal resident if it so chooses. Come on, where's your big scaley heart?" He shot his husband a tentative grin, which only made Mnth'rosfinn roll his eyes.

"Ugh, not those fucking hippies," was his only reply, but, with a sigh, he agreed. They then slowly began turning back towards their new destination, leaving Gh'reywinthx feeling distinctly smug.

Strangely enough, though, in Reptillica (the Reptillian language) the phrase 'Ugh, not those fucking hippies' sounded eerily familiar to the English phrase 'Let's just go back to our den and eat the girl'. This caused an immense amount of distress for Gemma, who was not very bright and simply assumed that the aliens were speaking English. What a moron!

In any case, she, in her panic, began flailing around and screaming for help, acts which the policereptiles mistook for signs of affection. Touched by the strange, vulnerable animal, they fondly huddled closer, secretly hoping that they could somehow keep the thing as an exotic pet, to add to their exotic pet collection. They were quite the intergalactic animal enthusiasts, and kept quite a few in their home, where they loved and cared for them tenderly and meticulously.

Coincidentally, their most prized creature was also from Earth: a small, hairless cat which had wandered into a void five years ago, on the outskirts of Toronto. They both believed it to be just about the ugliest thing they had ever seen, but they loved it more than they loved even each other. This was in large part because its particular brand of purring sounded like a strange, off-beat, incredibly emotional reading of a famous Reptillian poem. It brought them to tears every time, and it certainly impressed and awed all of their artistically-minded friends.

Gemma however, had meanwhile gone from being mildly anxious to experiencing a form complete and utterly paralyzing terror. She no longer had the mental strength to convince herself that her surroundings were merely illusory, The pressure of the situation being unbearable, the exhausted woman shut her eyes, and allowed herself to fall asleep, lest she sob like a child at the prospect of this nearly endless day (and with three suns in proximity to this new environment, it was, in near actuality, rather endless).

Gh'reywinthx and Mnth'rosfinn, as beings which did not sleep, believed that the creature's wavering consciousness could very well be a sign that it was close to death. They hence picked up the pace, hurrying towards the Refuge in their great desire to save what they hoped would be a prized addition to their pet sanctuary.

It may then be of some use to note here, that Reptillians had always been renowned for their incomparable speed. They were, in fact, regularly breaking the laws of physics through blatant disregard of the space-time continuum. This reality had actually led most - if not all - scientists to conclude that Reptillians were a myth. This belief of theirs eventually became so powerful that individuals born with excessive logical faculties had began to develop, entirely alongside their language skills, the ability to never see, hear, touch or experience the very existence of Reptillians.

Reptillians, of course, simply thought these people to be rather blatantly rude.

Luckily for Gemma, though, she wasn't one of those people. Hence, she and her carriers managed to arrive at the Refuge before they had even decided to head towards it. They rang the door, hoping for the best, and it opened quite promptly. The individual opening the door - an elderly Gorgonite Scientist - could not see the Reptillians and as such did not thank them for bringing the human to her door. The policereptiles, unconcerned, associated this with the woman's utterly over-exaggerated and somewhat bewildering excitement, exemplified by the large spiked protrusions which were beginning to sprout from her previously smoothened tentacles. A classic bodily side-effect of female Gorgonite's experiencing awe or excitement.

"Another human! George, George, dear Mathematics, there's another one! Can you imagine what this-!? Oh just hurry will you! This is going to be wonderful for my studies! Do you think it might be a female? It's definitely distinct from Augusto, but that may just be within the normal range of mutations - Oh this is just brilliant! How did it even get here? Another wormhole, maybe?"

As she spoke, clicking her tongue in her native Gorgon language, a second Gorgonite - her husband, George - arrived near the entrance. His excited allure was showcased by the colourful, feather-like growths rising from his greenish tentacles.

"Oh my, oh my Lord, Millie, this is so wonderful! Augusto will be so happy when comes back from his convention, tomorrow! Oh what if they become friends? And dear me, how rude, let us welcome our guests! Thank you so very much for bringing in the human, officers!"

The policereptiles, polite as they were, gleefully obliged while Dr. Mildred, George's stubbornly scientific wife, did not hear her husband's words, nor acknowledge the individuals brazenly walking into her home. Instead, she occupied herself by carrying the human into Augusto's room to rest. Meanwhile, George, excited to have new visitors, was whipping up one of his famous batches of Hewthfroth - a popular hot drink on Number Five characterized by the scent of green tea, the texture of maple syrup, and the taste of marmite.

The Reptillian couple sat down comfortably around the triangle dinner table in the quaintly lit, lilac kitchen while George got to work.

Dr. Mildred soon joined the lot of them, settling down and flipping through a notebook filled with equations. Gh'reywinthx and Mnth'rosfinn looked at eacho ther uncomfortably, wondering why the scientist was ignoring their gaze and refusing to make conversation. Finally, Gh'reywinthx shrugged, deciding that scientists were always rude anyways and that it was really no big deal. Or perhaps they were merely shy. Mnth'rosfinn, meanwhile, was boiling, but far too poised to say anything - especially when their other host had been so hospitable, but he sure knew that he would get a good rant about the whole experience later. Neither of them really ever understood what scientists were on about anyways: no Reptillian did. Having all collectively chosen to never abide by the concept of so-called 'reality', they saw science as a pointless and inherently restrictive set of laws, and as policereptiles, they knew that the only true laws were those created by their somewhat democratic, entirely capitalistic and vaguely fascist government. Nature and physics could go screw themselves.

Still, it was shortly after that George thankfully returned with four cups of freshly brewed Hewthfroth, and the Reptillian couple could not have been more thankful for his sweet presence. Mildred, of course, noticed only two of those cups, and reached for the one Mnth'rosfinn was about to grab, which caused him to gasp in audible frustration. Taking a deep breath, he settled for a different cup while Gh'reywinthx soothingly rubbed his back. Gh'reywinthx had always been the calmer of the pair anyways, there was little that could get under his scales.

"Please excuse Millie, she's so clever, she sometimes doesn't think about being polite."

Mildred was too lost in thought to hear. George smiled fondly at her and she swatted him away with an exhausted tentacle.

George cleared his throat before continuing. "Anyways, do you men have any idea how it could have arrived on Number Five? Millie, do you think it could have come along in the same way Augusto did?"

Dr. Mildred, unbothered by the guests she had no idea were even around, spoke without leaving them with any chance to put a word in, which was exactly the sort of behaviour that was beginning to really hurt Mnth'rosfinn's feelings.

"It might have," she started " I'll have to ask it some questions after I've inserted it with the microchip translator red ray thingie." The microchip translator red ray thingie, or - as the non-scientific population called it, the micro-translo-red-thing, being a standardized translation device named, produced and invented by Dr. Mildred herself twenty-five thousand years ago, and the reason why the two Reptillians could even understand a word of this conversation.

"I've actually" she continued, flipping through her notebook "been developing a theory according to which the wormholes first began operating from his origin planet around fifty Earth years before Augusto came along, due to some temporal disturbance that I haven't managed to identify yet. And since that time, their appearance may well have been steadily increasing in occurrence. If I'm right, we may well see more and more remnants of Earth. The theorem still needs work of course, but having a new specimen will be wonderful news for my research!"

Neither George nor the policereptiles quite understood what it was she was going on about, they nodded politely, in Mnth'rosfinn's case, in a desperate plea to prove that he was above all this. George and Gh'reywinthx on the other hand were really just genuinely polite individuals. Still, even Mnth'rosfinn had to admit that, despite Dr. Mildred's rudeness in doing so, it really wasn't so terrible that she was speaking over them and ignoring their presence. Not only were they almost completely unaware of the circumstances of Gemma's appearance, but they found the scientist incredibly boring, and it was a relief not to have to engage. They hurriedly finished their drinks before standing up to head out, which was a good thing too, as their nano bracelets had just started flashing red, indicating an urgent call in the agro-cultural sector of B-46K, which, as we all know, is quite a rough neighbourhood.

"Sorry to interrupt, Doctor-" Gh'reywinthx started, cutting off the scientist who was suddenly confused in the middle of her babbling, unsure of why she was stopping and unable to recapture her train of thought. "But we must be leaving. All we know is that she was found on the edge of the Flouffatron forest, by a farm in south Rickyville sector 137. We're sorry that we don't have more information for you both, but it does seem that the trespasser is in good hands. Do give us a call if you decide that the creature isn't intelligent and might need to be adopted, its head fur would contrast the blue walls of our living room just wonderfully! So, thank you for your hospitality, and for the delicious Hewthfroth, but duty calls, and we must depart, good day to the both of you!"

Gh'reywinthx then gleefully proceeded to leave George with his bracelet number and prepared to leave, prompting Mnth'rosfinn to merrily shake one of George's tentacles whilst giving the confused - yet unbothered - scientist a dirty look. They both prepared their departure quite rapidly after that. They got up and left only to disappear before they'd had time to sit down earlier in the chapter, they cleaned and put away their cups, pushed their chair back, and disappeared with no more tangible sign of their presence than the number in George's bracelet book. It all suited Dr. Mildred quite well, too, as she was getting tired from the exhausting act of not noticing the intruders.

Meanwhile, Gemma was just beginning to wake up, on a bed whose mattress and covers were sewed with a holographic fabric which at once reminded her of silk and rabbit's fur. She looked around to find herself in an immense, hut-like room, the walls made of jagged silver rock and above her stretched a wide, dôme ceiling of painted stars. She pushed a strand of hair away from her face, awed by the beautiful lighting bugs lazily floating around the atmosphere, nostrils fluttering at the gentle rose-petal scent clinging to her feather skin.

For the first time today, and for the first time in a very long time, she felt at peace.

This was, of course, merely because she was in Augusto's room, which had been carefully and scientifically designed by Dr. Mildred as a prototype of the perfect environment for human contentment. It replicated the most gentle, comfortable climate, scent, humidity, atmosphere and aesthetic for the human psyche, and provided a soft soothing noise which was imperceptible to humans by had a powerful effect on the subconscious mind, releasing pleasurable chemicals within the body, artificially replicating joy and drowsiness. It was only still a work in progress, which had begun when Augusto was first adopted and it had since continuously been updated, but it was nevertheless quite effective.

Gemma, pushed to the edge of the bed, wrapping herself underneath the strange and wonderful covers like a child, was in a state of bliss, completely unaware of the horror that Dr. Mildred was preparing for her in the neighbouring room, and uncaring vis-à-vis the oddity of her exhausting day. She deserved this room, after all she'd been through, and she deserved to have it without thinking about what it meant for a little bit.

So she was happy, while our favourite Gorgonite scientist was hard at work in preparing a complex machine in a cold, sterilized room, completely ignoring her husband's protests.

"Please try to be gentle with the human - Augusto was traumatized for so long after the insertion! Do you remember how scared he was of anyone touching his ear afterwards?" George had always been a sensitive fellow. Unfortunately for Gemma though, his wife was not.

"I have determined that the ear is the only proper port of insertion for this type of creature, anything else would either create an uncomfortable distortion of sound and space in the human's perception, or ruin their ability to speak at all! I will make sure to proceed with additional testings for this one, I hadn't realized just how fragile these creatures were when we first adopted Augusto. And this one has quite a different morphology, paler skin, orange hair, larger in height, but smaller in width, wildly different bodily proportions in several other ways… there's a chance that it could be sick. Or, female, or from a different climate, or on a different diet, it's really too soon to determine the exact cause of the visual discrepancies. In any case, it's definitely much older than Augusto was when he first arrived here. I just hope it isn't sick: I would hate for such a goldmine of potential research data to die before it stops being useful."

Realising that nothing he said could possibly change his sweet Millie's mind, George instead retreated to his observatory, overlooking their garden. There, he could focus on more appropriate and masculine concerns, such as the appearance of the lovely flowers in the garden, the shrinking lights in the night's sky, and the colours of the matter! Perhaps he might even pour himself a second delicious cup of Hewthfroth. It was only a small departure from his diet, so there was nothing specifically terrible about the idea.

Yes, he was almost sure that had read a study about how, secretly, Hewthfroth was good for the heart. His wife would surely disavow such a display of pseudoscience, but, well, if he listened to every one of her 'health concerns' he would never have any fun! Having firmly decided on his plan, he scurried back towards the kitchen to fix everything up. Soon, he would get to speak with a brand new human! And until then, he could relax: after all, concentration created wrinkles, and George took pride in his carefully smoothened tentacles.

Shockingly, while Augusto's room certainly had calmed her spirits, the unconditional terror resumed for Gemma when Mildred aggressively strapped her down onto a medical table and wheeled her into the next room. This condition was also, interestingly and coincidentally, exactly as harmful to the heart as Hewthfroth was. And the rapid, shallow beats were acting up again, pounding against Gemma's ribcage while she observed her surroundings in renewed horror. Above her was a hovering, large, bright white machine which was so complex that no possible amount of literary techno-babble could even begin to describe it. The room itself was no less intimidating, with shimmering white and reflective walls mirroring each other in infinite tandem, and a ceiling from which crawled uncannily moving, beeping, screeching metallic constructions, all working together in clicks and illusory twists, to break the schoolteacher's mind.

And it was effective. Dr. Mildred only appeared to the woman as a set of shifting, white, slimy, hairy, and surprisingly scaly tentacles which Gemma could hardly distinguish from the room itself. She was tweaking evil-looking things on the hovering machine, which, unbeknownst to the redhead, was not a torture device, but a large Sonar Distortion Insertion device. It had been designed by Dr. Mildred as a machine for the safe insertion and adjusting of the microchip translator red ray thingie, back when she was just out of University. For it, and for the accompanying microchip translator red ray thingie, she was a bit of a celebrity in the scientific community. This meant that everyone on the planet, and in the surrounding solar systems used her technology…

And that absolutely no one in the Universe knew who she was.

Nevertheless, the technology had been revolutionary at the time of its creation, causing a paradigm shift within the general population which was quite outstanding to admire. The device was, at its core, an attempt to eliminate all forms of miscommunication. As such, it did not merely act as a translator; it filtered the outside world into one which would be appropriately understood within the context of the individual's language. It may well be why scientists no longer saw Reptillians, and why children no longer understood their parents, but for the rest of the world, everything had become much, much more pleasant.

Unfortunately, Gemma's biology was resisting the treatment, and continued to do so, until an hour in, when it finally gave in, and the white terror-room slowly began to look like a classroom.

A Band Called The Electric Thumbs

Three young men in flashing outfits
Six chords over four
Pretentious smiles, oh what misfits!

The lights dim, the crowds quiet
And a true horror
Cynics petition in half a tormented riot

Why, oh why, would my son lend a hand
To this crappy rock and roll band?

When Life Hands You Lemons And It's Great Because You Actually Just Bought A Lemon Store So Thank You God!

It took three entire days following the procedure which allowed her to understand Fifthsonian speech before Gemma could finally accept the reality of her situation. Ot, at the very least, come to terms with the idea that, whatever hallucinatory delusion this may have been, it wasn't going away. Once that period was over and she was beginning to settle into her place on the couch in the corner of Augusto's bedroom, she managed to find a tool and a paper-like apparatus which allowed her to compile a top ten list of the useful and/or interesting information that she had managed to gather about this new world. Paraphrased, her list was somewhat along the lines of this one:

1. According to Dr. Mildred's data analysis, she had most likely fallen through a wormhole which brought her from her large metropolis in Northern Ontario to the countryside of the inhabited part of a planet called Number Five. Said wormholes were a reoccurring phenomena which linked various and seemingly points of Number Five and its moon back to Earth.

According to the scientist's calculations, they all linked back to the concentrated area of the Earth landmass known as the concentrated area of the Canadian province of Ontario. This, for no apparent scientific reason which the Gorgonite could muster as of yet, beyond perhaps the fact that it might actually liven up the place for once.

2. The inhabitants of Number Five were called Fifthsonians, and they generally found it very offensive when someone told them that the name of their planet was really stupid. Which was confusing because it really was a stupid name.

3. Only one other human had ever accidentally been dragged onto Number Five, as far as George and Mildred were aware. His name was Augusto d'Elea, and judging from what Gemma could glean from their admittedly short interactions thus far, he was almost as self-obsessed as he was idiotic. Yet she couldn't help but adore him for reasons she could not fathom.

4. Whatever horrible thing it was that they drank instead of tea or coffee, Hewthfroth, or whatever it was called, had to be poison. Gemma had never once tasted anything so vile, and she had once tasted her great-aunt's meatloaf, so she knew what she was talking about.

5. The only Earth-like fruits that actually grew on the planet were lemons. They had the exact look, smell, taste and texture, except here, they grew directly from the ground and were so prevalent as to be considered weeds. Gemma preferred the term "rare blessing".

6. The strange reptile creatures she dimly remembered who were always at three places at once somehow were probably a fever dream of hers.

7. The government was very extreme when it came to illegal immigration, the penalty for which, if improperly handled, was expulsion or death. This fact did not, however, scare her as much as it probably should have. It happened to be one of the very few

current problem of hers that she could even understand, and on Number Five, anything that made sense was inherently reassuring.

8. To avoid being brutally murdered by the government, then, she had to fill out paperwork. Which normally wouldn't be so bad if it wasn't in such an excessive amount that she had honestly and very seriously considered the alternative.

9. Gorgonites were terrifying to look at and unspeakably boring to talk to.

10. George-The-Gorgonite was just about the kindest being that Gemma had ever met, and she thought that was really nice.

These final two realisations had come as a great shock to Gemma, considering the outrageousness of their outer appearance. Strange, colour-shifting body modifications seemed to follow any emotional or intellectual response, and the schoolteacher was trying very hard to keep tabs on what they all meant, but it was considerably difficult.

Indeed, both of them seemed to shy away from vocalising their emotions, and they found it somewhat rude to be questioned about them. They both additionally seemed to have very separate bodily reactions in association to similar feelings. So far, she had understood that Dr. Mildred's - which always felt odd to say, perhaps because Gemma was used to formally addressed individuals having surnames, and Gorgonites had no such notion - skin started glowing when she was happy. George gre scales when he was flattered, and feathers when he was - it was either excited or confused. Feathers were somewhat ubiquitous on George's form, as was excitement and confusion within his psyche. Either way, Gemma had come to realise that their shape, though objectively terrifying, became, through prolonged exposure, comforting. And she was far too busy with the literal mounds of paperwork she had to take care of to be scared by tentacle monsters all the time.

God, that paperwork made her want to cry.

"Why in the holy god damned Universe is this form asking me to list my top one hundred and forty favourite colours in descending order of relevance? I- I don't even think I can name that many shades." She paused to ponder. "Is that something wrong with me, or is the question insane? No, wait it doesn't matter, this is totally irrelevant! At least on Earth, the irrelevant questions on immigration form are just racist and offensive, no one asks you to recite the expert version of a Sesame Street duet!"

It was unfortunate that Gemma Noelle Gott had decided to try humour out for a ride in a place where absolutely no one knew what Sesame Street was. Most of her material was made useless here. Helpfully, and easily ignoring the human's strange words, George spoke gently:

"Well, you do know that your colour preferences say a lot about your inner self! On Number Five, we find that quite important! It's something you'll learn soon, don't worry though, integration takes time, and I'm here to get you anything that might help ease the process!" He smiled, delightfully tapping a tentacle on her shoulder in an attempt at gentle reassurance.

"Oh, actually! You know who you should ask for help with that? Augusto! He's a great fan of colours, and he's so clever, he'd help you make the best choices!"

"Augusto? The poet? Yes, he sure seems like someone with the mental capacity to help with immigration documents! I'm not surprised that he's a fan of colours though. Somehow, it seems fitting.."

Thankfully, Gorgonites did not have a clear grasp of sarcasm. Hence, George only proceeded to tell her all about how glad he was that she agreed with him on this, and oh how much fun the three of them would have together! Gemma, groaning in frustration at the mere concept of what was happening to her, proceeded to knock her head down onto the desk multiple times.

"Oh Science! That doesn't seem healthy Gemma! Augusto never did that! Unless - Oh my is it a religious ritual of some sort!?" George feathered with excitement. "I do love religion! It's a real passion of mine, actually. You know, in college, I took a course in the sub-aerial religions of Northern Dervon - that's the country I'm from, on my native planet! - did I tell you that? It's also where I met Millie! She was protesting against the class being taught out of atheistic convictions." George smiled and shook his head, reminiscent. "It was love at first sight! - For me, anyways! It still took me quite some time to come back to my roots: that was all Millie! My mother was a very devout atheist, college was my rebellious phase. And even if I'm no longer of the Truther conviction, I'm quite glad I took the class that introduced me to it, who knows where I'd be if not for having met-"

"Is 'sun' a colour?" Gemma interrupted as she pulled her head from the desk, nursing a headache. This was the fifth time in three days that George had told her this story. She had very quickly learned to apply to George the skill that she had gleaned from teaching a class full of disrespectful children: voices are background noise. "Can I just name like- a bunch of things I know? Who even reads this?"

"Well - I don't know who reads this, but- and you'll find this interesting-"

She wouldn't.

"Augusto and I actually went to another colour convention, you know, for fans of colours? I don't know if I count myself as one, but I'm certainly an enthusiast! So yes, we were at this convention together a few months ago - different from the one he was at when you came here, but similar! Anyways-"

This was about when Gemma abandoned the form she could no longer concentrate on to resume her religious head-bashing ritual.

"At this convention - Colorama Major, if you're interested, they're actually holding a Colorama Minor just after the elections, it's going to be wild! So, what I was getting at, is that there was a very long debate there on whether or not each and every star should have it's own colour. Some people say it adds diversity and flair, and I think I agree with that, but the counterargument really makes you think, you know? Is it discriminatory towards the colourblind and the differently sighted to market such specific shades of colour? I can't say for sure, and honestly, I don't know that, as a person privileged enough to see colours with surprising accuracy, it's my place to say! I mean, I have never had to go through the troubles and pains of colourblindness-"

George kept going on the topic for about half an hour before he realised that Gemma had not, as he had mistakenly believed, entered the second portion of her religious ritual, compromising of near-absolute stillness, but instead simply fallen asleep on the table. This was unfortunate because, though George had no knowledge of this, Gemma was partially colourblind herself, and the insight she could have brought to the discussion was absolutely priceless.

The joyful Gorgonite was quite used to such disappointments, however: his voice had a soporific quality to it that both Gemma and Augusto were particularly sensitive to. He had, over the years he'd spent raising a human child, come to terms with it, and no longer found it to be offensive.

Instead, he carefully proceeded to carrying Gemma over to her couch, depositing her gently before covering her with blanket. Afterwards, he brewed himself a warm, well-deserved cup of Hewthfroth.

All in all, George was a pretty swell guy.

People... individuals? Aliens? Creatures? Fifthsonians probably? Nothing felt right- Whatever it was that Gemma was supposed to call the steady stream of various alien races that were always coming in and out of the Refuge... Fifthsonians were shockingly easy to get used to. As odd and jarring as life on Number Five was, after only about a week, Gemma was getting the hang of it. She had no control over anything whatsoever and just about nothing made sense, but it was all, well, colourful.

There was, for one, the constant presence of the bright pink, turnip-shaped and mouthless Thornbugs, creatures who communicated entirely telepathically. Though incredibly invasive, they were usually quite wise and generally good conversation partners. Most notably, Zena Perron was an eight-year-old, orphan Thornbug which George and Mildred had adopted after her mother, who had lived in the Refuge for months, passed away. While most Thornbugs had the politeness to catch her attention and give her some sort of warning sign before they broadcasted directly into Gemma's mind, Zena had no such qualms. She constantly frightened and shocked the woman: were children unnerving in every species?

Kalenworths were also a common and somewhat disturbing presence at the Refuge. They were creatures which looked somewhat like multicoloured, scaly cows, but who seemed to have been intellectually and emotionally stifled at the age of thirteen. They were not idiots, merely, they emotional, hormonal, incomprehensible, beings. Two of them, Yagen Worthfield and his girlfriend, Mogon Vinsproperl, were some of Augusto's closest friends, and spend quite a lot of time extensively discussing colours and wavelengths with him, an obsession which neither Gemma nor Dr. Mildred could properly understand.

And in between them and the numerous vagrant Whooldorths, Voloopsts, Growlths, Mousepatts, Dogthrists, Hoopstomps, Voopstomps, Mantispreas, Ghorlfordonts and occasional Gorgonites, normality was becoming far more shocking than strangeness. This had the unfortunate side-effect of turning paperwork into even more of a nightmare than it should have been.

So, at George's recommendation, in a desperate attempt to alleviate the difficulty of the situation, she asked for Augusto's help. Strangely enough, though she inexplicably found the man quite charming, his help seemed to make things worse. Currently, she was filling out a form and hoping to get his advice on the shocking amount of colour-related questions. Meanwhile, he wrote poetry.

"What do you think of this one? I find it quite expressive, don't you? It's so deep… I think it really reveals my inner thoughts and feelings."

The schoolteacher did not have time to respond before he pushed his notebook on top of the nonsensical paper she was filling out. She was unimpressed.

"You know, I don't think you're supposed to say 'fuck' in poetry." Was her only response, before pushing the thing away to focus on her work.

Frowning, Augusto looked over his poetry, seemed about to cross something off, then merely shrugged, putting away the book to glance at the piles of paper laid out before him. Picking one up excitedly, he started talking again:

"Be sure to fill in this one! It's super important! You know because it's printed on blue paper. Blue means strength, and importance. It's a very present, hot colour... Just like the fire it represents!" Fire was scarcely ever orange on Number Five, and almost always blue "But it's also soft... like the eyes of a wiseman... like my eyes."

Gemma was captivated, listening to Augusto. She shook her head when he finished talking, as if exiting a trance-state: His narcissism was infectious.

"Just- please, Augusto, just- stop talking and give me the papers. I don't know why I keep listening to your nonsense. You're a curse."

"Well, a great philosopher once said that 'Nonsense is just another word for truth.'" Augusto replied, feeling excessively well-spoken.

"Which-" Gemma didn't have high hopes for her ability to finish this thought uninterrupted. That was a good thing.

"The great Augusto Giovanni d'Elea! Poet, artist, philosopher, unpublished author, adventurer and future celebrity! I know, it's shocking, but it's true. I don't like to call myself a genius, but I suppose it's not fair to the others if I don't, right? If I try to convince my fans that I am an average man, then they may look at themselves and think 'wow, now if I cannot even be average, then am I no good at all?' That just isn't right! I could never cause the people such anguish!"

Augusto smiled, proud of himself, while Gemma rolled her eyes. Of course, she would be stuck on an alien planet, befriending the most obnoxious person to have ever lived.

"You know" she started, hoping to politely draw him away "I would greatly appreciate if you used of that great… selflessness… of yours, to help me finish these figurative mountains of paperwork I have to go through."

Unfortunately for Gemma, Augusto could never abandon someone in need. Hence, he perused through the stack of paperwork until he found a form that looked like it would be fun to fill out: And it was.

He of course did not realise that this particular page of his had been taken of the 'Optional' pile.

It was printed on neon pink paper and had numerous googly eyes glued to it which were meant to distract and enchant the individual filling it into absolute honesty. That was something Augusto could appreciate, as an advocate for truth himself. It also asked such crucial questions as "If the Universe is all powerful, can it make a burrito so big that it itself cannot eat it?" or "If you were a Gorgonite, which colour would you hope your surprise/glee feathers would be? *** Please skip this question if you are a Gorgonite yourself"

And of course, it featured the crucial "If Jo'hnny has three lemons and two of his friends would each like a lemon, how much of a dick is Jo'hnny for keeping all three, eating none, and throwing them in the garbage?"

The correct answer being, obviously, "Perhaps Jo'hnny has a few underlying issues which should be addressed by a professional. Issues which could explain and perhaps inform on a more acute level his current social interaction problems. In truth, someone ought to ensure that he is taken care of, and that everything is dealt with the respect and professionalism which Jo'hnny deserves. Poor Jo'hnny."

Poor Jo'hnny indeed.

Youthful Serenade

Crunched numbers in a silhouette
Of a brightened figure on the grand escape
A crowd shouts and stirs, grace and beauty in her pirouette
And her heart knows that her skin is but a cape

Red tie and a corporate smile
Television teeth cracked for a public worldwide
Empty words and promises dance in the air and fade in a mile
And half the world, but only just half stand by his side

The Electric Thumbs stoop low and snide
A soundtrack cut with teenaged cries
And their buttons stretch to hide
The lust and glutton trust in a bloody prize

And really, aren't they all foolish narcissists?

Well they are, but I am not.
Obviously.
Obviously not.

Jesus Christ, how could you even say that?
Projecting, much?

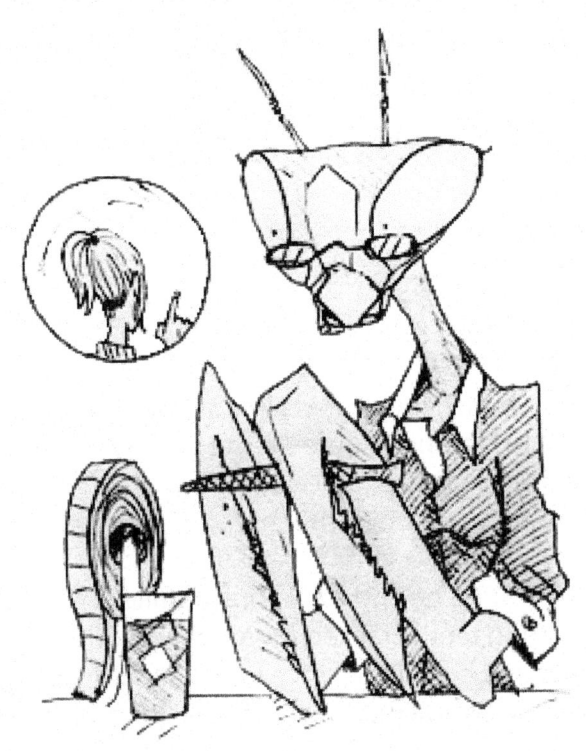

How Augusto Giovanni D'Elea Tripped And Made Someone Famous

"Can you tell us, miss, what your plans to fix the Fifthsonian economy are?" Asked the bored, furry, yellow mantis-like and rather feminine creature with gold-rimmed glasses who was interviewing a rather confused Gemma Noelle Gott. It was early that morning and, still in the comfortable pyjamas which George had sewed for her a few days ago, the woman found her face directly confronted with a circular piece of floating, reflective glass and an unexpected interview.

This was as average a morning as she would get on Number Five.

"Fix the economy? I uh- I really think you're asking the wrong person. I do not know how to do that. Especially not here!" Gemma responded, rubbing her eyes with her palm and stifling a yawn. She wasn't even fully aware of how their currency functioned.

The answer did, however, seem to shock the mantis woman into sudden interest. She paused for a moment, before starting up again, this time with renewed enthusiasm:

"Fascinating! Do you mean that financial experts should be the one to answer those questions, not a presidential candidate?" She seemed excited.

"Uh- Sure. Why not? -Hey, do you smell breakfast?" Gemma was used to being confused and surprised, she really was quite hungry though. Frankly, she thought that the bug alien and her floaty thing - which she knew she'd seen somewhere, if she wasn't so tired, she'd remember - but all that she really wanted to do was get to the kitchen. She was already salivating at the thought of her traditionally horrible morning cup of Hewthfroth (it was growing on her). She'd drink it with a side of fruits and woomp, woomp being a thick, sweet, creamy substance which perfectly accompanied and counteracted the acidity in her lemons and miscellaneous Fifthsonian delights. All in all, a wonderful morning treat which this stranger was depriving her of.

"Well, I don't know about breakfast, but otherwise, what a refreshing insight! I have to say, I've gone through over a thousand interviews today alone, of people saying the same things over and over again, and then there's you! How utterly bold!" She paused, revelling in her own dramatizations. "Now, I'm usually unbiased, but... Well gosh golly, I have to admit, I'm interested!"

She flipped through her notes with somewhat of a heightened air about her until she found what she was was looking for. The interviewer clutched the cue-card carefully, pushing the glasses up to her eyes with her large mandibles as she read:

"Alright, hotshot, you did well on the last question, but how about this: Can you detail your position vis-à-vis our current immigration policy?"

She looked quite proud of herself for that one too, before Gemma groaned audibly and forcefully: It was far too early in the morning for immigration policy.

"The Fifthsonian immigration policy? You mean the immediate murder or exile of all trespassers lest they find political refuge and fill out literal roomfuls- and yes, I do really mean literal - of paperwork ripe with pointless and, honestly? Weirdly invasive questions. I have never seen anything more ridiculous in my life, and I have just befriended a man who swears in poetry and once tripped and fell on the moon of an alien planet. Not to mention the other oddities I've seen which still don't compare to how incomprehensible the immigration platform is. Did you know that I live with famous scientist Dr. Mildred, whose technology is used by everyone in the galaxy, and yet no one knows who she is? How can you be famous without anyone knowing who you are, it doesn't even make any logical sense!"

Gemma had to take a moment, which was a good thing for the interviewer, who looked positively knocked off of her many feet.

"Well anyways, point is, yes, the immigration policy on this planet is the most ridiculous damned thing I've seen all week."

Silence.

"You are-" The journalist seemed to struggle to configure her own opinions on what the woman had just said. "So right!" She paused a moment longer, working out her own stupefaction. "Those immigration policies are in great need of change! ... Probably. And- Yeah, and scientists really should have more recognition! Wow- okay, yes, I've made up my mind!"

With a resolved look on her face, the creature turned towards the floating piece of glass and spoke decisively:

"People listening at home, I'm calling it right now, this-" She stopped, leaning over to whisper into Gemma's ear. "Uhm, sorry to be rude, what race are you exactly?"

"Human. Wait- listeners at ho-?"

"This- human, you said? Fun! And kind of exotic, if you don't mind me saying that - I just mean- I don't think I've ever met one of you before-"

That wasn't entirely accurate, not that the woman realised as such. She had, actually, spoken to Augusto on numerous occasions, without ever paying much attention to him. It appeared as though the Mantisprea - her race of alien, which happened to be dominant in the show-business industry - had a completely adverse reaction to Augusto, finding it difficult to register or remember him at all. That was, of course, precisely why he loved spending time with them so much: It was so refreshing! But it did mean he'd often been passed over for mediation opportunities.

"Sorry for that rambling, folks, you know me, I can't hide my happiness - that's trademarked Kuntz Gallows! But wow, dearest viewers, ladies, croaks, viles and gentlefolk, I never lie, and this human is going straight at the top of my list! And if any of you beautifuls know what you're doing, you'll vote for this - outstanding - human to be in the shortlist! And as always, let's give it up at home for our newest candidate in the running for the next presidency of Planet Number Five!!"

There was a distinct loud roar echoing from the glass, which then quickly proceeded to begin shrinking until it disappeared.

"Wait what did-"

"I am so sorry, I would love to be able to give you more time, but on to the next candidate! We have to be fair! Here, take my number though, trust me, we'll be in touch." Her face contorted into what Gemma believed was meant to resemble a smile. "See you around, sweetie!"

And on that note, she scurried quickly off, leaving a trail of golden glitter powder to float softly behind her moving figure. Gemma, on the other hand, was feeling demotivated, and was beginning to suffer from one of the splitting tension migraines which had been a characteristic staple to her past as a schoolteacher.

Thankfully, George was quick to bring her a warm, reassuringly disgusting (though she was admittedly beginning to take a strange liking to the substance) cup of Hewthfroth, accompanied with a flitter of the whiskers which suddenly adorned his face. The whiskers were a sign of concern, but Gemma was too shaken to take note of this new development on Gorgonite biology.

As for the explanation behind the somewhat alarming phenomena, well, considering the fact that here were several different ways to apply for a presidential candidacy on planet Number Five, as decreed by the Interspecies Comfort Equality Act, it took the lot of them - George, Mildred, Augusto, Yagen, Mogon, and the young Zena, all sat at the kitchen table - a full day of questioning each other, to truly understand what it was that had just happened.

A full day which was only interrupted twice. The first, by Yagen and Mogon's wild fan theory about the colour smaragdine having a corresponding sound quality which sung 'amaranth' backwards over and over again. Those were a confusing and boring few hours. And the second, by Augusto forcing everyone to read a new poem he'd just thought of, to which Gemma had to react, deadpan: "Poems usually have words, Augusto."

Augusto did not change his poem, but in an effort to please his audience, he scratched out a few words at the bottom of his already perfect, wordless poem. He hoped that didn't make him a sell-out.

Of course, the interruption was made all the more annoying once they realised that what had transpired was all Augusto's fault. Not that anyone was shocked by the revelation. Because, obviously, it was going to be Augusto's fault. The Universe constantly revolved around Augusto Giovanni d'Elea's bastardly whims, fancies, tastes, thoughts, and glittery nails.

Augusto had never had to fill out any paperwork; George generally and very graciously did it for him. An act which didn't seem to accrue much, if any, forms of protest from the young human. Hence, he was exceptionally bad at it, and the single paper he chose to fill out for Gemma just so happened to be a political application form. One which was meant to be filled up by individuals willing to apply for their candidacy to be considered for presidency. Nevertheless, while the subsequent interview had been highly alarming to the woman, the whole situation did not seem to be treated like as much of a big deal for everyone else.

In truth, she was mostly nervous due to having never been on television. And of course, this strange alien device which periodically appeared in front of bored Fifthsonians was even more nerve-wracking than the primitive earthly device she was used to. As an illegal immigrant, she did not have access to her own Glassbot, but she didn't think that she would ever even want one: they creeped her out a bit. At least on earth people had the decency of hiding their computers and televisions in their own house or, at the very least, in their pockets, or discreetly hidden from view. These devices were, quite simply, just far too social for her liking.

In any case, beyond her anxiety pertaining to the thought of her image being in the public sphere, neither she nor the rest of the people in the house were particularly worried about the potential outcome. This was, of course, only the first draw: Anyone could enter it, and as Gemma was informed, they would receive a two-minute televised special, and the population could then vote for their favourites. The ten individuals which had accrued the highest number of votes then became official presidential candidates. Considering the fact that there were hundreds of thousands of individuals applied to be in the first running, the chances of Gemma going any further than that were extremely thin.

Getting a shout out from Kuntz Gallows, the Mantisprea presidential interviewer, was however, at least according to Augusto, a real honour, and sure to bring a fair bit of attention her way. Still, Dr. Mildred was quick to dismiss her worries:

"Gallows is an airhead, everyone with half a pear's braincells would know that she has absolutely no idea what she's talking about. She has influence, but, statistically, her words might really only sway some 32% of voters, according to my estimate. Most of which are Mantispreas themselves or youngsters. I wouldn't worry about much more than being approached to star in a reality show."

Augusto gasped, shutting his poetry book in absolute excitement;

To see his newest friend realise his dream of being part of a reality show was the next best thing to doing it himself! Mogon and Yagen leaned in, more invested than they had been all evening. Before any of them could say anything, though, Gemma weighed in:

"No offense, Dr. Mildred, but wouldn't it be much simpler and less stressful to just... Retire my application? Or leave? Abdicate? Honestly, anything would do... what do Fifthsonians do when they change their minds about wanting to be president?"

Dr. Mildred rolled her eyes, annoyed, while George rolled a soothing tentacle around his wife's neck, choosing to speak on her behalf. In truth, the Refuge was George's passion, which he had transmitted onto Augusto. While Dr. Mildred enjoyed the concept of bringing help to those who need it, she often found their guests bothersome, and she especially had little patience with creatures who didn't have working knowledge of Number Five's political system.

"Well, darling, they don't change their minds. That's illegal. And honestly, since you're already technically not supposed to be allowed to be on Number Five, at all, you really should follow the laws carefully... If you do it could actually speed up the immigration process though! A lot of individuals chose to do this, it shows that you're politically invested, that,s a good thing!" He paused, his tentacles shafting into scales of discomfort for a second. "Well- I mean, there is a possibility that they'll interpret it as an attempt at a coup for the sake of your home planet, but I really think you're probably going to be okay."

He smiled reassuringly, and Gemma shivered: Gorgonite smiles were utterly and chillingly terrifying. Unfortunately for the woman, the young Zena, sensing her anxiety, started singing soft songs in the redhead's mind to help calm her down. Which of course was overwhelming and somewhat stressful, but the ex-schoolteacher didn't quite have the heart to let the child know that their efforts were vain. Instead, she whispered a gentle thank you towards her, which Zena giggled at: forms of gratitude were rare and somewhat embarrassing, in her language.

George, realising that bringing up the possibility for a miscommunication, while it was meant to be kind may have somewhat unnerved the female human, also tried his hand at calming her nerves.

"Really, I do mean it when I say I wouldn't worry too much about it, though darling. I mean, the presidents have all been Theobite aliens. Forever. Since the beginning of Number Five. Well- since the beginning of the post-colonial era of Number Five. In any case, you're a human, you have no chance."

Gemma, with her bright orange hair, and weird, mushy human eyeballs, was sure to alienate the majority of the population, even if she did have the approval of the notoriously odd television host. This reality, surprisingly, did not allow Gemma to lose her steadily rising desire to brutally murder - or at the very least seriously maim - Augusto d'Elea for getting her into this situation.

How ironic, that she was already thinking like a politician.

Trumpet Sound

pfwaa
PFF
PFF
pfwaa
PFF
PFF
PFWAA
pfWAAAAAaa
PFWAAaaaaaAAA
PFWAAAAAAAAA
PFWAAaaaaaaaA
PFaaaaaaaaaaaaa
PFWAAAAAAAAA
BWAAAAAAAAAA
pfwaaaaaaAAAAAA
pfWAAaaaaaaaaaa
PFWAAAAAAAAAAAa
PFWAAAaAAAaaaaaaaaaaa
PFWAAAAAAAAAAAAAaaaaaaaaa
pfWAAaaaaaAAAAAAAAAAAaaaaaaAA
PFwaaaAAAAAAAAAaaaaaaaAAAAAAAAAA
pFwaaaaaaaaaaaaAAAAAAAAAAAAAaaaaaaaAA

PFwa
PFWAAAAaaa
pfWAaa
pff

(I have never played the trumpet before)

(but I think I killed it)

How Gemma Noelle Gott Tripped And Made Herself Famous

Nothing made sense. Ever. And it had taken Gemma a surprisingly short amount of time to accept the fact that what little control she used to have over her life had completely vanished. Thirty days prior, for example, she had been the victim of a random televised interview caused by Augusto d'Elea's mistake. Since then, a flurry of journalists had been in and out of the Refuge to interview her. Not to mention the fact that Dr. Mildred had begun testing out a new flavour of Hewthfroth, which everyone had to suffer through. It tasted better, but the change was unpredictable and just all around awful.

And somehow, despite this Hewthfroth catastrophe, she had become the first non-Theobite candidate to reach the top ten in the last millennia. And of course, the very first human in all of Number Five's history to have achieved such a feat: it was a very big, completely unwarranted deal. On the other hand, this also meant that there was an entire army of top tier lawyers suddenly taking an interest in her immigration case. One good thing in an ocean of terrible, but it was still a little bit worth it.

Gemma Noelle Gott had not touched a single piece of paperwork since the announcement of the results, five days prior. Neither had Augusto, for obvious reasons.

The free publicity was also, of course, an extraordinarily good thing for George and Augusto's business, the Refuge, and for Zena, who quite enjoyed being able to broadcast herself into the minds of everyone who owned a Glassbot. And while it had taken a while for the Mantispreas to acknowledge it, Augusto's on-screen magnetism was was undeniable.

This was also why Augusto had become somewhat of a manager for Gemma. It worked too, while he and his Kalens friends were busy distracting the public through colour conspiracies, loops, hoops and subtle advertising, Gemma could relax. Sort-of. Augusto's advertising of the Refuge as the solution for the poor, the hungry, the homeless and the dramatically underdressed was bringing in crowds of new individuals to the place. He, Gemma, Zena, George, Dr. Mildred, Mogon and Yagen all now shared a room together out of necessity, which was making the place quite cramped.

Still, what had started out as a great amount of stress was slowly turning into a treat for the schoolteacher and her entourage, what with everyone bending over backwards to please them. George had a million people to listen to his stories, Augusto's poems were starting to get some serious attention, Yagen and Mogon were getting signed to a label for their new band, 'The Sound of Smaragdine', Zena was slowly becoming the child all Fifthsonian children look up too and everyone suddenly seemed to love Gemma Noelle Gott.

The only one who wasn't at all pleased by the new development was Dr. Mildred, who was outraged that a woman who had absolutely no knowledge about, well, anything pertinent to life or politics on Number Five had gotten so far in her presidential campaigning on a platform of nonsense. Not to mention the fact that the Glassbots floating around filming and taking pictures were invading her scientific process and often making a key part of her study, Gemma Gott, completely unavailable. As such, the Gorgonite scientist regularly came across as rude onscreen, especially when layered with her husband, who was always regularly supplying the staff and crew with 'Newthfroth' the nickname they gave to the new Hewthfroth flavour which George and Gemma were both admittedly trying quite hard to get rid of as soon as possible. Still, it seemed nice, and the scientist seemed mean, and that was all that anyone was concerned about.

And really, what was this Dr. Mildred doing anyways? She was working on some kind of study about something-atmosphere, something-the steadily increasing number of asthmatic refugees, something-wormholes, something-Earth, something-blah, blah, blah. Nothing this boring could possibly be worth being so rude about. So, while Dr. Mildred was getting up in a fuss about clinical environments, standardized testings and room contamination, everyone else thought she really ought to relax and have a little fun for once.

And Gemma was one of them. Everything was terrible, out-of-control, messy, wild, weird, awful and incomprehensible, but she could finally just lay back and let it all happen. After years of teaching ungrateful children and getting verbally abused by their parents for it, she could enjoy a bit of a break. So, she decided one night to sneak out of the house by the window, thus avoiding the reporters. And along with her on this mission to explore the Fifthsonian nightscape, she brought one very anxious Augusto who questioned just about her every move.

"Are you really sure about any of this? I really don't think mum would approve." He hissed between clenched teeth, clutching the edge of the windowsill.

"Just jump, Augusto!" She laughed, folding her arms across her chest, staring at him in disbelief. "You're an adult, you can do this. Hell, I used to do this kind of thing all the time when I was a teenager. Come -on! I just need a tour guide that won't put me to sleep." Gemma egged him on from below, green eyes staring upwards, her feet firmly planted in the gelatin-ground. The ground which, it turned out, was of a rather pleasant texture when one had the right shoes, and the motion was quite soothing. All things considered, it was probably an improvement on its earthly equivalent.

Augusto took several deep breaths, trying to calm himself down. He was never a rebellious fellow, and this was quite stressful to him. Finally, he realised that this was the only way for him to be a gentleman, and took the inevitable plunge down the three and a half measly feet that separated the window from the ground below.

"See, that wasn't so hard, was it?" Gemma smiled, joking around while Augusto huffed.

"Well you're lucky I'm a gentleman, because what you're trying to make me do is just insane. Seriously insane. It's-" he leaned in to whisper, "disobedient."

Considering that most of the legal penalties for breaking Fifthsonian law involved either death, banishment, or in rare cases, both, she supposed it made sense that Augusto had been brought up to fear civil disobedience. Regardless of personal background, such consequences were enough to make anyone nervous. If Gemma became president, she vowed to herself that she would change that: Not that she wanted to be, but if it happened… well, what was the harm?

The past few days had been overwhelming, yes, but also quite a thrill for Gemma. When she spoke, people listened, people cared, her words had an effect, her expressions were scrutinised and internalised: She had, somehow, turned into an Augusto d'Elea, and the feeling was intoxicating.

Energised, she rushed forward, forcing Augusto to catch up behind her while she admired the view of the open field behind the Refuge. The sky was a rush of purple and orange in tangled webs of patterns, and the trees in these areas were white as snow and full of vines. The wind tasted scarlet and the gelatin-grass grew fuschia. When Augusto caught up to her, she spoke:

"You know, I think I get it. The obsession with colours on Number Five. Everything is just… brighter? I guess? I mean, damn… Earth just feels... grey next to this. No wonder the people here grow up to revere colour."

Augusto smiled a goofy smile, hands in his pockets while he walked next to her.

"I don't know. I think it's just because they're really controversial, I mean people love to argue, right? And everyone has a favourite colour, so everyone's wrong about what the best one is, and if everyone else is wrong, then you're just really smarter than the rest."

Gemma couldn't help but laugh: there was something magnetic about the man, something oddly charming about his simplistic, nonsensical meanderings.

"You know, sometimes I almost think you're smart. That charm of yours is really blinding."

He shrugged.

"I am smart. I mean, teachers don't usually think so, but I am. You people are just really weird... You know? Like you all need to put words in a big box and make them make sense. Speaking of which, will you be a teacher here? I mean, that could be cool, right? Think about it, you could teach earth history and you wouldn't even have to be right, everyone would just believe you! Even I'd believe you, honest, I was really bad in history. You could tell them about like... Godzilla or something, they'd think your planet had some kind of encounter with God, they'd be so jealous... Come to think of it I'm a bit jealous! Why do Earthlings get Godzillas, that's not even close to fair!"

"You say 'Earthlings' like you're not one of us." She laughed, "don't you ever... you know, miss it? Your friends, your family, everything you ever knew... Godzilla... Or honestly, even just other people?"

He shrugged. Again. He seemed to do that a lot.

"Well now I really do miss Godzilla. I can never watch that movie again. Ever. In my life... I could make it though! Ohhh, with a Reptilian as Godzilla! Well, I dunno, that might be a bit unrealistic, most Fifthsonians don't even believe in Reptilians, let alone Godzillas... not a great plan. Or- A great plan. I haven't decided yet."

"Okay... but what about the rest?" Gemma found it difficult to believe that Augusto could possibly have no attachment to earth beyond, well, Godzilla.

"Nahh, I don't think I actually care much for humans - uh, no offence!" He paused to look over, trying to make sure that he hadn't accidentally offended the human he was walking with.

"None taken." Gemma had never been a huge fan of humans either.

"I mean, my parents were great, but I don't remember them that well anymore. I used to miss them a lot, my first few years here, but then there's George and mum, and they're the best parents I could have asked for. So I mean, it's all the same, anyways, isn't it? You see people or you don't, but you always kinda just see them at the same time. Like- They're just far, they're not dead. Or they are dead, but I don't know that, so they're never dead, right?"

Gemma turned slowly towards him and arched her eyebrows in amused incredulity.

"That made absolutely no sense. And... thanks."

"You, my friend, are very welcome. Augusto the wise always knows just what the right thing to say is."

"He sure does. Word on the street is, he's an idiot, though."

"Well, I think you really need to check your sources on that, professor."

A Band Called The Electric Thumbs II

Trashed motels and sex on the plane
The drugs are life, love, to the band
Terrors covered in screeching feign
Thumbs are on electric demand

Ten trees sliced into pocket green
They reek of marketable greed
Though without something to mean
Too bad, they have got all they need

They've got the ripped tight jeans
They've got the white powder
They've lived beyond their means
They're too far to wonder

They are assholes
They've got gold soles
Their mothers are drowning in payrolls
They are so proud of their son's sold souls

ARE RELIGIOUS FREEDOMS MORE IMPORTANT THAN SPIRITUAL RIGHTS? A PHILOSOPHICAL LAWBOOK

The Presidential Debate was a very big deal on planet Number Five. The ceremony opened with two hours of poetry readings. It was a rousing, pandering, exciting competition that usually resulted in at least four deaths per event. This time, there were six registered deaths and at least fourteen life-threatening injuries: it was a good one.

Behind the scenes, Gemma was getting ready for her debate by having Augusto install the traditional presidential flower-crown on her head.

"So, it's just talking right? I won't be surprised with a- fist fight to the death in the middle of the procedures or anything?" She spoke with an only haphazardly nervous voice while she examined her freshly manicured hands for any imperfections.

"Nah, the deaths are only in the openings: Poetry can get pretty rowdy. The actual debate part isn't as exciting, which is why it's after.

The parents can put the kids to bed once they've seen all the exciting parts, but at the same time, so many people are tired out from all of the excitement that they're too lazy to change the channel on their Glassbots." Which, Gemma had finally come to understand, functioned as phones, televisions, computers, cameras, and gaming systems.

Or, in Earth terms: phones.

"So anyways, it really increases views! God, I wish the poetry lasted longer though. It's really wonderful to see other artists practicing your craft, and these are the best! You know it did used to be longer, too, but activists thought it was too violent and just forced the government to have it shortened by protesting... It's a shame really. I mean, back in the good old days, four years ago, things were a lot better! Anyways, good luck tanking this, candidate number eight! Don't accidentally become president or anything!" Augusto laughed nervously: If he was honest, he was becoming more and more worried about Gemma. Over the past few weeks, she had seemed to take an increased liking to her new situation. He just hoped that she wouldn't actually go through with any of it.

And, completely ignoring Augusto's slightly shocked and desperate attempt to say something, she got up. He couldn't believe how easily she shrugged him off, like he wasn't even there. He spoke with a few distant waves, and she completely disregarded him, running on stage before the announcer finished naming the candidates, causing a sea of cheers from the surprised audience.

"Well it looks as though we've got a change in the form, this year!" Yelled out the announcer, Kurtis Gallows, Kuntz' very well-known brother. "So let's give it up for all our candidates! Jed, Fed, Led, Ted, Ded, Yed, Hed, Gemma Gott, Med and Sed! Come on stage everyone!"

Crawling behind Gemma, a neat, steady line of eight seemingly identical starch white toad creatures wearing flower crowns and nearly identical angular ties in various shades of indigo-blue, walked in: Theobites. Augusto had been right: blue was a powerful, yet gentle colour in the Fifthsonian mythos. They all settled in front of their particular posts, seeming startled by the excitement of the crowd: generally speaking, by the time they had come on stage, most of the thrill built up by the poetry readings had died off, and the Mantisprea animator struggled to keep their attention. Not this time: Kurtis was having the time of his life with the crowd.

"What a fantastic audience tonight! As you all know, this is a historical election!" The cheers of the audience intercut his words, which he seemed both surprised and incredibly pleased by. " Not only is this the first time we have a human in the running: Gemma Gott, who was discovered by my lovely sister, Kuntz, but we also have our youngest Theobite candidate in history, give it up for Med, who is only twenty five thousand and three years old!"

The noticeably wrinkled and greying alien waved enthusiastically and twisted his mouth into what Gemma assumed was supposed to be a smile.

"Well, without further ado: let's begin the debate!" Shouted the announcer, revelling in this newfound power of attentiveness from a crowd which was habitually unresponsive.

As was expected, none of the questions made sense to Gemma, which began as a frustrating endeavour, but slowly turned into an advantage: Every ignorant, undocumented, contradictory, made-up comment of hers caused a huge riot in the audience. Kyle, the Gorgonite mediator, Kurtis the animator, and every other live or on-line commentator extrapolated meaning that wasn't there in her long-winded, nonsensical speeches, which was fun for a while. And when she grew tired of making things up, Gemma simply started giving out the absolute opposite opinion to that of all of the other nine contestants. Towards the end, it became not a question of winning or losing, but a quest to see how far was too far in Fifthsonian politics. It seemed as if nothing was off the table, which was somewhat surprising considering the contestants had a knack for arguing about subjects on which they appeared to have the exact same beliefs.

The first question had set the tone for everything that was to come:

Kyle the mediator cleared his voice, suddenly solemn as he spoke to the contestants.

"Well, Theobites, human, our first question tonight is a difficult, controversial one, brace yourselves, because we are digging directly into those hard lines: What should be the official Fifthsonian colour? DISCUSS!"

Through the gasps and murmurs of the astonished crowd, the contestants began shouting out their opinions:

"Indigo!" "Cyan!" "Celeste!" "Teal!" "Blue!" "Azure!" "Turquoise!" "Ultramarine!" "Sapphire!"

And as they continued on, speaking over each other and arguing about shades of blue, Gemma defiantly yelled out her own opinion, trying very hard to keep a straight face as she did:

"Orange!"

The shouting stopped, the crowd gasped, slipping to the edge of their seats: No presidential candidate had ever dared to bring up such a controversial colour as a suggestion. Orange was a statement. Orange was a declaration. Orange was a rebellion.

And Gemma Noelle Gott was leading it.

"Wow. Unexpected to say the least... What boldness, let's give it up for candidate number eight, breaking the mould! Candidate number four, care to offer up a rebuttal?" posed Kurtis, slowly recovering from the shock.

"Uhm- Why yes! I believe that to suggest such a colour is to show great oversight of its offensive nature. Historically, we are all aware of the suffering of the proud Flogborth nation, and the pain which this colour brings them. In fact, the very colour of the fur on your head is enough to make me shudder: unless of course, this is due to a medical problem, in which case, do see me very apologetic." Jed, the fourth candidate, nodded solemnly, and so did the rest of the

49

Theobites. Their nods, however, while distinctly in opposition of Gemma, were also obviously lacking in support of each other.

There was, after all, a genuinely subtle art to nodding, one which Gemma did not seem to understand, as she shrugged barbarically. This action caused, as any civilised individual would expect, a brand new wave of shock within the audience.

"Oh now, now, let us not resort to obscenities, candidate number eight, this is a distinguished organisation! Long gone are the barbaric times of shrugging and quiet contemplation competitions. We Fifthsonians are an evolved people."

Still, Gemma was making an impression. The following question was one which questioned the current laws regarding religion, spirituality and philosophy, and whether or not they deserved to be updated to better serve the people of Number Five:

"We need better religious freedom laws, I am horrified that we don't already have them! Everyone should be able to practice the religion of their choice without discrimination!" Croaked Ted, who was horrified.

"I find that offensive! What we need are better spiritual right laws! Everyone should be able to practice the spirituality of their choice! You don't care about the people, I am appalled!" Croaked Jed, who was appalled.

"You both disgust me! Number Five needs strengthened philosophical entitlement procedures! I cannot believe you both would have that overlooked!" Croaked Med, who was disgusted.

"I say ban all religions, spiritualities and philosophies! Or let them be! Who needs them? Not us, and yes us! They're ridiculous, and we love them like that! Or! We! Don't!" Gemma cheerfully replied.

The whole stadium exploded in sounds: cries of approval, frustration and opposition were thrown her way, and she fed on that energy: How bloody miraculous was it that her completely unthoughtful commentary hailed such reactions!? She had been an idiot for spending so much of her time trying to craft intelligent, meaningful, thought-provoking lectures for her class of inattentive, idiot children and their PTA parents. Here, it didn't matter: everything she said was made of gold.

The other candidates chose not to comment on the issue.

An Original Lose Vong

I S(ee)?
Si.
IS(ee)

IS I?
S- si

forgise my audacity,
and my mixing my s and my v
(pleave lose me)

Mo' Money, Mo' Sweet, Sweet, Stuff

"Would her honourable madame president, Gemma Gott please step forward for the official signing ceremony?" bellowed a very well-adorned Kuntz Gallows who had been newly surgically enhanced with shiny silver mandibles. She was enjoying the fame which came attached to her new promotion as an Official Executive Presidential Promotional Agent. Indeed, after the result of the vote saw Gemma Noelle Gott becoming the new president of planet Number Five for the next seven years to come, the ex-schoolteacher had found that there were no anti-corruption laws to stop her from hiring whoever she wanted, in whatever made-up position she so chose. She had vowed thus forward to elect all of her friends in positions of power, and as such, in part due to Kuntz' mediatic force, the presidency had become somewhat of a game show.

A large percentage of the Fifthsonian population truly admired this policy of absolute transparency which allowed them to see and understand the inner workings of the political system. Others, however, found it disgraceful to see important policy-enforcements reduced to the proceedings of game-like mechanics. The presidential channel on the Glassbot was less than tasteful and highly staged, but unfortunately, the outcries came from a minority of individuals which were easily dismissed, especially for Gemma. After all, if the entire world was concerned with mere artifice, why shouldn't she deal in it? Appearances and superficialities were currency on Number Five and Gemma Noelle Gott was the richest woman alive.

Thus, she stood forward and bowed for the crowd, for the camera, and for her Official Executive Presidential Promotional Agent. Kuntz then slipped the comically intricate, golden, jewel-adorned ceremonial crown onto Gemma's head. It was very much in motion, quivering, like swirling tentacles above her head. As Gemma waved proudly to the crowd, the Mantisprea bent down to whisper into her favourite human's ear.

"Today's a really big day, we've got a huge crowd, like something we've never seen before! I think word of mouth is really spreading: So good luck girl!" The satisfied Mantisprea pulled back and struck a pose behind the president, grinning widely.

Honourable President Gott cleared her throat and smiled in a pause, waiting for the audience to follow the instructions as exposed in bright, flashing letters above her head, just out of shot of the Glassbots: SILENCE. When the crowd began to hush itself, she spoke.

"Today, ladies, gentlefolk, Gorgons and other peeps, today my dearest Fifthsonians, TODAY! Is a historical day. Indeed, from this day forth, upon the signing of this document and until the end of time, or the point whereby someone else changes it back, the official, national colour of planet Number Five will be true orange! Or, as some would call it, colour wheel orange! Hex triplet code #FF7F00, for the incredibly precise!" Though Fifthsonians had no knowledge of hex triplet code, the micro-translo-red-thing allowed for everyone to understand within their own codified systems the specific measure of shade to which Gemma was referring.

The crowd's reaction was mixed at best: though she had several supporters, spouting big orange clothes printed with the slogan that had grown attached to her: "Take Back The Wheel! The Colour Wheel That Is!" there were also an impressive amount of very loud protesters. They were a various grouping of strange and diverse aliens in shades of blue, holding catchy signs with slogans like "Orange You Tired Of All This Nonsense!?", "Blue-Us Back Together!" and "It is our constitutional right to decide of our own national identity and a foreign leader who won by a flimsy minority of votes should not make life-changing choices for our nation that the majority do not agree with!" Which admittedly fell a bit flat in English, but was quite moving in Kalenorg. And of course, in Kalenorg, it rhymed.

Gemma loved all of it. The good, the bad, and the incredibly sweaty. All of it. She almost loved the outrage more than the support: What power! To have such importance that her most haphazard of throwaway thoughts could cause individuals to feel angered to the point of taking the time not only to think of slogans, but to make signs, clothing, and to oragnise staged protests! It was unlike anything Gemma could possibly have imagined.

She smiled to her population as she signed off on the new bill, and in the back of her mind, she dreamed of the delicious feast and wonderful cup of what she now called "Oldthfroth" that she would be having that night: catered by her own personal Official Executive Presidential Chef.

Helen from the PTA could suck it.

Augusto was walking in circles in Gemma's office, a few minutes after the room had been cleared out, post signing, and she sat, staring at him blankly. She waited for a few seconds, hoping the disturbance would just go away. And when it resolutely didn't, she dragged an enormous sigh. Finally, her honour spoke:

"Augusto, hey, man, Augusto, I don't mean to be rude, but also can we speed this up a bit? You said it was an emergency, remember?" Her honourable presidency could not quite remember why she had appointed Augusto as her Official Executive Presidential Office Managing Supervisor, but it probably had something to do with the fact that it was a very important sounding titled which meant very little in actuality. Either way, she wished that the poet would speed up whatever it was he was trying to say to her, because she was getting bored, and she was quite hungry.

And if this had anything to do with that new Glassbot show of his that had premiered last week, 'Augusto Shouts', Gemma thought she might go insane. It featured him, Mogon, and Yagen reading and performing Augusto's awful poetry, and talking about their irrelevant opinions. The show featured such hit topics as: colours, textures, lights, patterns, the socio-political treatment of immigrants, smells, feelings, shiny things and matte things, all of which were equally inconsequential. The result was something which was strangely captivating, highly addictive, and absolute garbage, according almost everyone else who had ever seen it. Almost. According to the new Fifthsonian president, it was merely boring.

He seemed hesitant, as though lost for words.

"Listen, and don't take this the wrong way, I'm glad you finally have all those people listening to you-"

"Finally!?"

"Yes, -finally- you have all those people listening to you. And all this great food and no more paperwork, and stuff like that, but don't you think you've taken it far enough? You're the president, you can change the law and excuse yourself, you don't have to do this anymore. Why are you-? What I mean to say is that all those new bills are really upsetting to a lot of individuals, and the national colour... Well colours are really important here, you know that! I mean, remember our talk? It's kindof a big deal."

"Augusto: You are an idiot." She sighed, annoyed. "Colours are cute, but they're pointless. I changed the national colour, and a bunch of people are acting like children. This whole thing? It's a joke. It's thrilling, and it's hilarious, and everyone is going insane over the least important thing I've ever done. I made it easier for immigrants to move here, I changed the penalties associated with minor crimes to soften them, I'm a good president. Now if you'll excuse me, I'll be wearing my brand new, orange, designer dress to my amazing feast, like a true Fifthsonian patriot!"

The president lifted herself off her chair, ready to have Augusto dismissed.

"But you're not a Fifthsonian! You've done some good things, but you have no idea what life is like here. Crime rates have gone up, and those criminals are sentenced to jails that don't exist, the population has skyrocketed, there's a housing crisis, and people are marching down the street to protest. I'm not saying it's all bad, but you can't just mess with everyone here. You don't get why some things, like colours, are a big deal. Or why they mean so much. They just do. Just-" She wasn't listening. "This is really important, don't ignore me!"

Gemma stared at him point blank:

"Sometimes, important things are ignored."

She turned, and she left. And she didn't notice when someone burst into her office, coming face-to-face with a startled Augusto, mere seconds later.

Her Little Drummer Man

Come, my mother told me
Be the dream I've always wanted
You'll be their newborn king, just see
And you'll have all I've ever needed

Pa rum pum pum pum

The finest gifts they'll bring
For their everything, my dear
They'll lay before their king
And you'll never bear a smear

Pa rum pum pum pum

So to honour You, no poor boy can
Spend to hear the gift of their king
You'll play, my little drummer man
And make me rich, with what you bring

Pa rum pum pum pum

Then they'll smile for your solo
And your sick drum flow

Pa rum pum pum pum

Religious Folly And Ah, Fuck

The creature that entered the room mere moments after Gemma's exit, when Augusto was sat discouraged, humming a song from his childhood, was a thing unlike anything he had seen on Number Five. It was the strangest, least comprehensible thing he'd seen in years: an incredibly old, grumpy-looking man, dressed like a cliché, with a deep coarse voice and a London accent.

"Lord, do you need an improved security system, this old piece of horse crap is riddiculously easy to break past. Listen- Oh, yeah, I know, shock! Gasp! Whaat? The whole bloody shebang. Another human on Number Five? Yeah, well, it hasn't been long, and it won't be much longer, I like my ground rocky, not jelly-like thank you very much. I'm Theodore Smith. Doctor, Theodore SmithI've been living on the Fifthsonian moon for about forty years, I'm a million bloody years old, and until about a week ago, I was pretty damn sure I was the only human in town. Now, how did you and queen orange bitch make it here? Because if it's anything other than an Ontarian wormhole, I can go back to my bloody home. If it -was- an Ontarian

59

wormhole though... Well, I think we're all fucked."

Augusto stood shocked, unable to respond for quite some time. When he finally did, it was to stammer something about how he should really talk to Dr. Mildred, his mother about all this, and to mention that he himself, Augusto d'Elea, had a lot of new poem ideas and really, really needed a nap.

Dr. Theodore Smith was not impressed.

———

Gemma had fired Augusto that night after her feast. Or rather, she had asked Kuntz to fire him for her, but neither he nor Dr. Mildred seemed to have gotten the message, as they all obsessively tried to reach her. She was, as it turned out, far too busy to deal with their petty nonsense, and Augusto had had her attention the last time he had cried "emergency" to no avail. That morning, she especially didn't have time for any of it, as she rudely hung up on Augusto.

Her Honourable Madam President was having a large and rather important dinner with the Head Priest of the Truthers, the most prominent and influential Fifthsonian religion, which stipulates upon the existence of planets One through to Four, despite lack of scientific evidence. The Head Priest has contacted Gemma with rather interesting theorem: He very much believed that planet Earth, Gemma's home, was the sacred planet Number One, blessed it be. And more importantly, he believed that she, as an immigrant of that planet who had risen to fame and influence, was The Chosen One, the alien to save Fifthsonians from certain doom.

Gemma, as it turned out, liked that idea very much.

"Sir Clint Nau, Head Priest of the Truthers, newly appointed Official Executive Reverential Religious Leading Associate has arrived! Shall I install the Glassbots?" said Kuntz Gallows, dramatically bursting into Gemma's office in extravagant golden jewellery and surgically-enhanced, silver-plated antennae.

"Lovely! Bring him in! And of course! We can't have such an important meeting without it being streamed to the global population!" Gemma had grown quite fond of herself as an onscreen persona. "Just give me a makeup touch-up first! God, I'm so relieved Augusto isn't doing that anymore, he was good, but have a great eye for detail, Kuntz!"

Kuntz was not as good as Augusto. But she worked better when she was flattered. The Mantisprea smiled and blushed, getting to work:

"All of this" she directed her front legs over her highly retouched, shimmering mantis body, pointing herself out "is all thanks to you, Madam President. You and that lovely raise you gave me when you had me take over Augusto's responsibilities. You will have the best hair and makeup ever, I mean, "Go orange!" right?" She giggled, carefully pinching open a makeup bag.

"Plus," She added, clipping open the foundation "I think 'Augusto Shouts' is like, way overrated. He is so uninteresting and boring! All of my Mantisprea friends agree, too. I mean, you're the magnetic one, I really don't get what anyone sees in that human boy. He is so dumb, unlike you: everyone knows you're a genius."

Gemma smiled, content, and refrained to comment until Kuntz was done.

"You look so good I could just eat you up!" She chirped cheerfully "I'll just let him right in!"

Only a minute or so later, sir Clint Nau, Head Priest of the Truthers, newly appointed Official Executive Reverential Religious Leading Associate was walking into the president's office, followed closely by a crew of Glassbots. Clint Nau was a particularly tall Gorgonite who was sprouting extremely colourful feathers of what Gemma assumed was excitement. He was, interestingly, the only recorded Gorgonite in history to have a surname: Clint had always wanted to leave a name to his descendants, for prosperity's sake (his children should know that, despite the uninspired 'Nau' he had chosen to pass on to them, they came from greatness) he had thus chosen to legally change his name to include one, back in his early thirty thousands.

"Oh my, your Honourable President" he started "your Orangecy, if you will, you are even more stunning in person than through Glassbot. If I do. Say so. My-self."

She blushed. "Oh, sir Clint Nau, Head Priest of the Truthers, newly appointed Official Executive Reverential Religious Leading Associate: you flatter me! Come, let's talk!"

And talk they did, about how the Gorgonite was, upon meeting her, now convinced that she was the Chosen One. About how if Gemma would only spread the Truther religion to the masses, and open up their eyes, they could work together for a better future. For a better Number Five. Gemma was almost convinced, and she was just about to steer the conversation towards a theological conversation about wealth (she didn't want to promote something that might be damaging to the economy, after all, rich people were an important and oft misunderstood kind), when Kuntz Gallows burst into the room in a panicked state.

"I've turned off the Glassbots in this room and sent out an interrupted signal message, turn your personal ones to channel forty two! Augusto Shouts is on, and miss Honou- Gemma, Clint, just watch this. It's just bad press, it's really, really bad press, and worse news. This is a national emergency."

And so, they turned their Glassbots to channel forty two, Augusto Shouts, where Dr. Mildred and a strange, horrifying, bizarre, grumpy, extremely old scientist man were doing what scientists do best: ruining everything for everyone all the time.

Wonderful.

———

After ordering a shut down of Agusto Shouts for unlawful propaganda, Gemma "invited" (the word 'ordered' just seemed so harsh) Dr. Mildred, Dr. Theodore Smith and Augusto d'Elea for an emergency meeting. Along with them came George, who brought Oldthfroth, and Mogon, who was complaining on behalf of herself and Yagen about their segment on colour-coordination in the fourth dimension being cancelled without reason. Yagen was just too upset to come.

Dr. Mildred was scaled with absolute anger, and Dr. Smith did not seem much happier to be meeting the President. In fact, it was fair to say that positively everyone, including sir Clint Nau, Head Priest of the Truthers, newly appointed Official Executive Reverential Religious Leading Associate, who was feeling a little jipped by the whole sequence of events, was a bit on edge.

Except George. George just brought the Oldthfroth: he was in a pretty good mood.

"I cannot believe you would discuss high security governmental matters on an unlicensed Glassbot show! You should be executed for treason! And you would have been if I wasn't the president. Any other would have!

Dr. Mildred scoffed.

"I have been trying to speak to you about this matter for weeks, this was the only way to get your attention, and you didn't even let us finish before you cut us off! At least now we can talk, as I repeatedly mentioned: this is urgent."

Gemma only rolled her eyes, and it was Dr. Smith who answered in lieu of a far too frustrated Mildred.

"Well, Madam Goddamn President, what we were about to inform the population is that we've concluded that it was I who caused the temporal rifts between Number Five and Earth. They started when I was trying to invent time travel, a very, very bloody long time ago, when I had a lot more patience in me. The problem is, that they are increasing in frequency. This wouldn't be a huge problem, more of an inconvenience- bringing in more of your lot in here and forcing me to wander off a perfectly wonderful moon-, except that they absorb carbon dioxide from Earth's atmosphere. I'm not sure how planet Earth has fared for so long with the wormholes absorbing such large-scale amounts of the toxin from its atmosphere, but I do know that this is what's made so many Fifthsonians fatally ill. And by that, I mean that over a billion Fifthsonians have already been affected by this. About sixty eight percent of Fifthsonians are hypersensitive to the molecule, it's quite important that something be done of it, and religious babbling - offense intended mr. Clint - aren't going to do the trick."

Sir Clint Nau, Head Priest of the Truthers, newly appointed Official Executive Reverential Religious Leading Associate literally bubbled in utter outrage and shock, but before he could rebuke the elderly man's offensive words, Gemma spoke, frowning:

"Can we do anything to stop it?"

Mildred sighed.

"That's just the issue, Gemma. The only way to stop the progression is to stop the temporal rifts - the wormholes that is, and the only way to stop them is to destroy their point of origin."

"You mean…"

Dr. Smith, cold and harsh, was the one to answer:

"To save Number Five, you have to destroy planet Earth."

Plastic Orchestra

tic, tock, tip, top, toe
a metronome beat
lick, lock, lip, lop, low
a falsified sheet

and ahoy goes
the plastic orchestra
and their plastic woes
follow their plastic formula

flick, flock, flip, flop, flow
a string quartet fleet
pick, pock, pip, pop, poe
a crucified meet

and ahoy goes
the plastic orchestra
and their plastic foes
in true neon nebula

sick, sock, sip, sob, sow,
a counterfeit treat
dick, dock, dip, drop, doe
a genuine cheat

THE RISE AND FALL OF QUEEN ORANGE BITCH

The emergency council was built out of a group of strange and diverse individuals which were meant to represent Number Five as fully as possible. Gemma Noelle Gott was there for her role as president, Dr. Theodore Smith and Dr. Mildred were meant to explain and deconstruct scientific inquiries and bring forth solutions to their environmental crisis. Augusto d'Elea, Kuntz Gallows and Kurtis Gallows were there to discuss media strategies. Sir Clint NauHead Priest of the Truthers, newly appointed Official Executive Reverential Religious Leading Associate was to offer up a religious viewpoint on the situation. Jed and Med, the Theobite brothers who had become co-leaders of her opposition party were there to provide opposing political outlooks.

And of course, George and Zena were there for the cookies.

"These cookies are delicious." said George, and his daughter nodded in approval. A loud 'They really are, I love them!' then reverberated in everyone's heads, courtesy of the seven-year-old telepath.

"Yes, yes, dear, the cookies are great, they aren't exactly the matter at hand though." Mildred had been annoyed for the past week. She was frustrated by the fact that organising a crisis conference apparently took so much time. Mostly because it didn't usually take that much time. Gemma needed time to recollect herself if she was to avoid panicking at the conference, which was that she wasn't convinced she wouldn't be doing anyways.

"So," the Gorgonite scientist continued, "I propose the swift, quick and painless destruction of Earth. We have interplanetary travel technology and nuclear power of the necessary volition, there is absolutely no reason to delay this any further. I understand that this might be a sensitive subject for some of you, but it's a simple matter of survival. Ours, or theirs. If we could engineer a solution which would cater to both planets, we would, but it's far too late. That would take years of research at which point we might be looking at an inhospitable Number Five. It's the only way. That is all. It will be quick and absolute, Number Five won't have any negative repercussions, in fact, the population need not even know."

Outraged, sir Clint Nau, Head Priest of the Truthers, newly appointed Official Executive Reverential Religious Leading Associate stood up to respond:

"No repercussions!? Do you have any idea what you're dealing with here? Planet Earth is the one true planet. It is planet Number One, and Madam President Gemma Noelle Gott is the chosen one, she will save us. To destroy planet Earth would be to commit a terrible mistake: if we are to live beyond the grave, we must sacrifice ourselves for its survival."

"Far be it from me to agree even in the slightest with Saint Lunatic, but we cannot dismiss the environmental and societal impact that we would be inflicting upon the world. Planet Earth is just a planet, really, nothing special, but it does contain life, and we are talking about absolute genocide of over eight point seven million different lifeforms, we cannot brush this off." contributed a very downtrodden Dr. Smith: as much as he found most everyone here irritating (except for Augusto, who was strangely charming, and Zena, who was just absolutely adorable), he had to admit that even he didn't know what the best course of action was.

Gemma was trying very hard to remain calm.

"The strange creature with the white hair has a good point." Jed started. Med continued: "Yes, any rash action could lead to an international dispute of unprecedented proportion, the best thing to do would be to do nothing. And use this time to find a believable cover story to calm the population down after that stunt. If the population is occupied, we might find a solution to the problem, or a cure for the ill. A good many Fifthsonian species are built for this kind of thing, everyone in this room- well" Med paused to glance uncomfortably towards Zena, who was gleefully and telepathically devouring cookies. "Well we're all fine now, so it's a non-issue."

"We could cover it all up pretty easily, I caught them quite quickly" Kuntz pitched in, her brother nodding in agreement while Augusto looked uncomfortable and fairly upset. "We do this sort of thing all the time in the industry, really we don't even need to lie, just- redirect public attention. We find some other news story, bank on it, cover it wall-to-wall, and no citizen will care what anyone said on Augusto Shouts, and every journalist on the planet will be too busy trying to get a leg-up on the story to even remember what happened. It was a fluke. No harm, no fowl."

Dr. Mildred was offended:

"You people are idiots. Or you're all insane. We cannot sit idly by. We cannot waste our time fooling the population while we have a real crisis on our hands-"

"Why?" Gemma was finally speaking. "I mean, so what? If we do nothing, we save a planet, and sure, we sacrifice a few lives along the way, but people die no matter what we do, right? What's the difference between not telling the population and letting them live in- I don't know, blissful ignorance?"

"No, information is always better." replied Dr. Smith.

"Well, in that case, couldn't we- tell Earth? If we can send something to destroy it-"

"At great economic cost!" interjected Med.

"Sure, but if we can destroy it couldn't like- send a ship, take all the people at least? Then it's not as cruel."

"Take the humans where exactly? We don't have that kind of land or those kinds of resources. We can send a bomb, sending a fleet of ships is something completely different."

"I'd like to reiterate that, while the Chosen One would know best what the correct course of action is: whether planet Number One is fated to sacrifice itself to the good of Number Five, or whether it be the other way around, it is my professional and religious opinion that Number One, as home of the sacred, should be preserved, and that it is a grave mistake to be so selfish as to appeal to the Chosen One's sensitivity towards other creatures for our own benefits: we have used, we have abused, it is our time to give back to that which has given us life."

He nodded profoundly to himself. George seemed compelled by this answer, perhaps a remnants of his rebellious teenage years, but no one else seemed to be particularly interested in what he had to say. Even Zena, had stopped eating cookies to pay attention, curled against a defeated Augusto, she tried to hold back tears. Jed and Med were cold and impassive. Gemma was paralysed. Neither Kuntz nor Kurtis seemed to know very well what to feel, Dr. Mildred was still furious, and Clint looked like he wouldn't mind someone dropping his titles today. So, n an attempt to distract from this religious nonsense, Dr. Theodore Smith looked Gemma in the eyes and said this:

"Ultimately, it's your decision. I sure bloody wish it wasn't, but legally, it is. Still, I highly recommend you make it quickly: this problem is only going to get increasingly worse, faster, and unlike a few others here, I really don't recommend doing nothing. Honestly with careful planning and 'great economic cost', it might be possible to send one large ship, pick up a few thousand people, which should save humanity from complete extermination. But it's not perfect. You're still exterminating millions of lifeforms, the humans would be hard to accommodate on Number Five, there's chances of retaliation on their part, and ultimately it still means choosing who gets to live and who has to die. "

Gemma sighed.

"All right, call up the Glassbots, and draw up a crowd, I know what to do when I have no more viable options. I'm an elementary school-teacher, goddamnit."

A Band Called The Electric Thumbs III

Was it ever really about the music?
for years we played in our parent's garage
but I throw my nose at a bad acoustic
you spend your time on a groupie's corsage

You piss me off with your flightless blonde
I throw you off in our hotel bar
you call me up and I don't respond
I mess you up and you're still a star

Don't think I'm fucking nostalgic, why would I
miss the nothing we've built for fame
I poked my own skull for a golden eye
but fuck, our music is so goddamn lame

Doesn't it freak you out that we've gone this far
I never shed my soul, my tears, my fears, my goal
and neither have you, but we sold a branded cigar
so it's done: there was never a thing in this whole

We built our songs for teens to love
A killer hook and meaning devoid of

yeah, that's all,
that's it for us,
fuck the band called

The Electric Thumbs

Epilogue: It's All On You, Now

Gemma cleared her throat and stepped up towards the Glassbots. She shook nervously, as she looked over the buzzing crowd of orange and blue. She paused, took a deep breath, and smiled when she spotted Augusto looking up from his seat to give her a double thumbs up. She wasn't sure when he had stopped being upset with her, but it felt nice. George was there too, next to him, sat cozily wrapped in a blanket with Zena, whose voice croaked quietly at the back of her mind:

"You got this. Probably. I mean, I know, I'm seven, maybe you're stupid and going to kill us all or something and stuff. But you let me eat all the cookies at that meeting and I actually kinda like orange, so- you're probably doing fine. Anyways, don't be nervous, people are just gunna be mad at you like always again. It's no biggie."

Gemma thought that was pretty wise, so she opened with that:

"I'm not a very smart person. I used to think I was, when I was a little kid, mostly because no one liked me very much, and I guess I could count pretty well, and I guess I could read pretty well, and few teacher told me I was probably a bit clever. So I grew up with all those great big thoughts in my head thinking I was some kind of genius and if someone would just listen to me, they'd know. But then it turned out that reading and counting were pretty much the only things I could do pretty well, and those things only get you so far when you're pretty terrible at everything else and it turns out you really aren't that clever after all.

So I stayed in school because I was pretty okay at those things, and I studied to become a teacher because I didn't know what else I could ever possibly do, and no matter what, I kept thinking if only someone would just- just listen to all my great big thoughts, I could change the world. And so I started teaching and it went okay until it went terrible, and I realized that none of those kids were listening to me at all, and even if they were, all they'd ever learn was reading and counting, but I convinced myself that was just because it's what they made me teach. And then one morning I fell on another planet and became an illegal immigrant. Yeah, I know, it's pretty weird. Well, some genius or something filled out an application for me to become president and somehow, for the first time, and in a way that was entirely out of my control, everyone was listening to what I had to say. I could spill every great big thought in my head to nine billion lifeforms and all of them cared. I didn't even have to try, really. People got angry, passionate, happy, and every stupid thought that ever crossed my head was the most important thing in the fucking universe. And that was amazing. And yeah, I said 'fucking' in a speech, and fuck you too, let me meander on until I get to the point.

So anyways, I think I got a bit caught up in all of it. I mean, who wouldn't? Because who the hell thought it was a good idea to give this much power to just one dude? Maybe there's a reason Theobites always get elected. I'm not saying they're good presidents, they're awful and stale and gutless, scheming bastards, but they're these near-immortal assholes. Or they are actually immortal, maybe. Shockingly, I know absolutely nothing about anything in this world: Why do all the Theobites I've ever met have three letter names that end in ed? Is that an offensive stereotype or is it part of their culture?

I genuinely don't know, and honestly? A big part of me doesn't care. But for some reason, a lot of you guys like that. Which I guess is how I got elected, sensationalism and a good marketing strategy, thanks Kuntz! Anyways, it's been fun fucking around, but something came up that I really do care about, so- this is going to get weird.

I arrived on Number Five through way of a spontaneous wormhole: it appeared under my feet, and I wound up strung up in a tree. Uhm- A few religious people think that's- fate, I guess, but I don't. The scientists I've talked to think it's all because of some really, really old English scientist with a bad attitude and a flat on Ontario. Which- means nothing to any of you, probably, I don't know, maybe the micro-translo-red-thing made that work for you. But it makes a lot of sense to me. And it doesn't really matter much what you believe because the fact is that those spontaneous wormholes are increasing, and they're dangerous, and apparently they're making a lot of you sick, I'm sorry about that.

I don't- really understand the details, but the smart ones here are handing out pamphlets, and anyone at home can find the information on the official government website. So, apparently, the only way to get rid of those wormholes for good and stop them from releasing more carbon dioxide into the Fifthsonian atmosphere is to destroy the source of the temporal rift: planet Earth. My home.

And I'm supposed to be the one to make a decision on that. As I could ever be objective on the subject... We could do nothing. Let the innocent people of Earth live their life, and suffer through some of the potential losses. I mean, sir Clint Nau, Head Priest of the Truthers, newly appointed Official Executive Reverential Religious Leading Associate thinks that it's the right decision, and that Earth is the sacred planet Number One. They think it's worth the sacrifice. And to be fair, it could be. Not everyone there's like me, there are some damn brilliant people over there as well, so I don't know. I don't think it's a sacred planet, to be candid, but it could be. We've already established that don't know anything about anything, so- ...

Well... we could, potentially save a very small fraction of the popula- tion, but that would come at - as Jed and Med would say 'great economic costs', and, more importantly, it means we have to decide who is saved, and who gets to stay behind and die off. It seems like the best option, but it's complicated too, and I don't know if I can ask you all to do that for a population that you have never met. Who am I to say those things? I'm just one person. One stupid person, too. But I have to make a decision, and it's so much pressure, because suddenly, out of nowhere, every one of my big thoughts count and I don't think I'm well equipped to deal with that. I don't think anyone, Theobite or not is well equipped to deal with this either. How is it fair to turn people into Gods?

Or maybe it's just me. Maybe it's just me who's too weak to handle that type of thing, and there are some who really do know what's best for everyone, and maybe even if there isn't, there exists some perfect, magical system that can replace whatever the hell we have and make it better for all of us. But until then, we have this, and we have me. So- this is what I've decided to do. Tomorrow, I'll be holding a vote. Everyone over the legal age of adulthood according to their species has a right to cast theirs. And if they chose not too- Well, I guess that's a vote in and of itself. There are going to be deaths no matter what, and large societal costs. Some are going to be more affected than others and it won't be fair. But whatever happens from now on, it's on you. It's on all of us.

So we'll be a planet full of goddamn murderers, and whatever we decide, I guess we deserve each other."

Character Index

Ded (mr.)- Theobite, 77,321 years old.
    Politician

d'Elea, Augusto Giovanni (mr.) - Human, 27 years old.
    Poet/ Promotional Agent/ Glassbot Show Host

> George [Adoptive Father]
> Mildred [Adoptive Mother]
> Zena Perron [Adoptive Sister]

Fed (mr.) - Theobite, 73,400 years old.
    Politician

Gallows, Kuntz (mlle.) - Mantisprea, 136 years old.
    Glassbot Reporter/ Promotional Agent

> Kurtis Gallows [Brother]

Gallows, Kurtis (mr.) - Mantisprea, 147 years old.
    Glassbot Show Host

> Kuntz Gallows [Sister]

George (mr.) - Gorgonite, 55,448 years old.
  Refuge Owner/ Househusband

   Augusto d'Elea [Adoptive Son]
   Mildred [Wife]
   Zena Perron [Adoptive Daughter]

Gott, Gemma Noelle (mlle.) - Human, 36 years old.
  Elementary School Teacher/President

Ghhrths, Gh'reywinthx (mr.) - Reptilian, 34 years old.
  Police Officer

   Mnth'rosfinn [Husband]

Ghhrths (née Tryhgv), Mnth'rosfinn (mr.) - Reptilian, 28 years old.
  Police Officer

   Gh'reywinthx [Husband]

Hed (mr.) - Theobite, 62,046 years old.
  Politician

Jed (mr.) - Theobite, 65,046 years old.
  Politician

   Med [Brother]

Led (mr.) - Theobite, 38,001 years old.
  Politician

Med (mr.) - Theobite, 25,003 years old.
  Politician

   Jed [Brother]

Mildred (dr.) - Gorgonite, 55,448 years old.
  Scientist/Inventor

   Augusto d'Elea [Adoptive Son]
   George [Husband]
   Zena Perron [Adoptive Daughter]

Nau, Clint (sir) - Gorgonite, 53,457 years old.
> *Religious Leader*

Perron, Zena - Thornbug, 7 years old.
> *Child*

>> Augusto d'Elea [Adoptive Brother]
>> George [Adoptive Father]
>> Mildred [Adoptive Mother]

Vinsproperl, Mogon - Kalens, 1,001 years old.
> *Glassbot Show Animator*

Sed - Theobite, 42,781 years old.
> *Politician*

Smith, Theodore - Human, ??? years old.
> *Scientist/Mysterious Other Jobs*

Ted - Theobite, 52,750 years old.
> *Politician*

Worthfield, Yagen - Kalens, 1,000 years old.
> *Glassbot Show Animator*

Yed - Theobite, 64,322 years old.
> *Politician*

SPECIAL THANKS

To the many brilliant teachers who, over the years, had faith in me and my goals, and who made me grow as a writer and as a person *Colleen Ayoup, Chrystine Bleau, Lucie Bernard, Thomas Fisher, Philippe Gendron, Jason Katz, Jean-Marc Leduc, André Matteau, France Riquier, Daniel Stefik, Yvan St-Pierre*, and almost certainly more.

To my loving parents, who have always pushed me to be the best that I could be *Irene Rossaert & Eric St-Georges*

To the friends who dealt with my incessant need to bother them with questions and my own self-doubt *Michael Ceasare, Jean-François Dumont, Lianne Graham, Quincy Jackle, Rachel Lalonde, Brigitte Papadakis, Maxine Peseke and Bryn "Hunter" Thompson*

To my friend and illustrator, the wonderful *Ioannis Lazaras*

To the two brats who constantly challenge me to be a better person, and who I actually do love more than anything in the world *Samuel Collette & Satteva Olatunde*

To my immensely large family who has always supported me in my insanity. Especially to my cousin, *Magali St-Georges*, who knew I would be a writer before I did.

And to *you*. For reading this dumb book about aliens that I care about too much.